A Battleaxe and a Metal Arm 18:

Across the Ashen Sea

Samuel Fleming

Cover Art by David Leahey

ISBN-13: 978-1-954679-52-8 (paperback)
ISBN-13: 978-1-954679-51-1 (ebook)

Thank you to my Beta Readers

And, as always, to my First Reader,

Mel.

iv

Contents

"That I should walk long after
my brethren have gone…
That is my damnation."

—Unknown

Previously...

The heroes stepped onto a moss-covered realm lined with streams of glass. At first, the appearance had belied an easy journey, but it wasn't to be. They walked across the realm seeking the seam and the feeling of souls—the same as when they climbed the Godpeak. Souls were coalescing, flowing into the streams from other realms. And with them, the sense that the missing souls of Accaelum were there too.

Remnants dotted the marshy landscape—outlines of buildings, monuments, Terrans, and creatures. Streams grew more numerous, thickening into strange rivers filled with the souls of the long dead.

This was a feeding ground. One of the central realms of Sala Gahenna—the heart of the dungeon. The closer they trekked to the center, the more the realms would break down. The stranger the realms would become.

As they walked, the heroes bonded over living through others. Shawn lived through dreams. Taunauk through his shieldbrother, and Helesys through Aradi.

The first true creatures they encountered were ethereal spiders. Giant arachnids that could disappear from the realm and reappear a moment later. Shawn told Helesys and Taunauk about the one he'd fought beneath the wizard's tower. The resulting battle was hard fought. Helesys used fire magic and burned down the dying forest, and walled off the other side of the river with her Ring of Winter. In the end, Taunauk used his ancestor's power to see into the ethereal realm and see when the spiders would reappear—he slaughtered them easily.

Next, the heroes follow the river of souls to a set of massive obsidian pyramids. Around the base, they met more strange, horned Terrans, like those from the hills beneath the Godpeak. It echoed a warning to the heroes before disappearing in a flash of leaves.

Before entering, they talked of the Gatekeeper, and how they thought she'd been usurped and corrupted by the Wolf King. That she was the mysterious Voice at Meridian that had gifted them the power to bring back things after death. Taunauk and Rehkoros had a moment together—a small mend in the rift between them.

Finally, the heroes entered the howling pyramids and stalked through the dark halls. In the middle, they were attacked by marionettes reminiscent of those in the ruins of Antrikaumora. In the absolute silence, Helesys could not use most of her spells, but she was able to conjure her arcane blasts and slices of fire without words—by sheer will.

When the heroes emerged from the pyramid, they found the glass river deathly silent. The souls had been pulverized by the strange machinery inside the pyramid. Ground down to essence.

The heroes feared for the missing souls of Accaelum.

They found a black monument, and beneath it knelt an old foe—the former green knight—now given themself to death and destruction.

The knight challenged them to battle, but Taunauk challenged her to single combat. Powers of death clashed with souls, darkness clashed with life. Taunauk's rage proved too much for her. In the end, the knight and barbarian met with one desperate clash. His ancestor's power, magnified by a father's anguish and a son's rage—

Taunauk nearly cleaved her in two.

In the final bounds of the realm, they crossed a deep gorge—the final gasps of the river of souls. They poured through cracks in the glass into an abyss—

Into something too terrible to look upon.

Beyond the gorge lay the dried desert of the realm. It was there that their faith was rewarded, and Taunauk found the ten thousand missing souls of Accaelum. They flowed into Taunauk, and their power was nearly too much for him to bear. But finally, the golden glow faded to a smolder.

In time, the burden would be easier to bear.

The heroes walked further, passing through a weakened, almost nonexistent seam, and emerging onto a shore where glass gave way to ash.

~ ~ ~

Cape of Ruin

A desert of glass gave way to a realm of shadow, ash, and death. Helesys pushed aside as much of the darkness as she could, compounding and flaring her *warding light* until it reached jagged mountain peaks in the distance. Just before that, the shadows churned like inky water.

But she could already feel something pushing back against her power… Her light was fading. The mountains disappeared into the oppressing gloom. So too did the silhouettes of monsters and otherworldly creatures.

Helesys strained her power against it, but her *warding light* spell had its limits. Whatever force pushed against her, it was beyond her power. And Helesys suspected she knew what it was—

Sala Gahenna—*the dungeon*. They were walking into the heart of madness. Where the Wolf King dwelled—the usurper.

Helesys finally relented, relaxing the Gar of Shéslang. Her light faded, receding till it stretched only a few dozen feet around them. Pitiful in comparison, but the oppressing darkness relaxed as well, as if it took pity on them. Like they were a jester walking humbly through a court.

Helesys had been so consumed with the spell that she didn't realize Taunauk and Shawn were eyeing her.

Shawn asked, "Are you alright?"

She nodded. "We'll have to make do."

Shawn shrugged. "Better than being underground."

Taunauk grunted and readied his axe and shield. He was still glowing with the might of his ancestors. "I can see. The way is clear for some time. We may need your water walk spell though." He didn't elaborate further.

Shawn muttered. "Nothing worse than an ocean at night."

They walked across the ash field, power kindled and weapons ready.

~

Ash stretched out into the shadows.

Periodically, Helesys flared her light, pushing the darkness back to glimpse anything that might be hiding. It wasn't long before they saw the land sloshing—it seemed as if they walked across an inlet or land bridge, beset on either side by dark water.

But at a glance the water looked no different from the land on which they walked. Both were the same black and speckled gray of ash.

Helesys paused and walked to the edge of the solid land. Then she dipped the butt of the spear into the water, prodding the bottom but found none. She leaned closer, pushing the spear as deep as she dared, and still touched nothing.

"Don't fall in," she muttered, pulling the spear back. The water dripped from its surface like sludge, but fell away cleanly.

Taunauk turned to Shawn. "What manner of creatures could live here?"

Shawn feigned surprise. "Why are you asking me?"

A long bellow echoed across the realm—no doubt one of the serpents they'd glimpsed in the distance.

"Because you know more about strange realms than we," Taunauk added.

"Oh… I suppose you're right." Shawn rubbed his chin. "Things that are powerful, strange, and ancient. Things without souls or that are too stubborn to die."

Taunauk grunted. "Things we should avoid."

Shawn scoffed. "I would say so."

Helesys turned, leading them along the shore—if it could be called that. "Did you meet anything like that in the dream realm?"

"Occasionally. Old gods. Creatures from other realms. But really, it's hard to say. It's hard enough to remember things from my time as a wisp. Even if I did meet something like *that…*" he said, gesturing across the black sea. "The stranger the creature, the more unknowable it is, and the harder it is to remember. I couldn't tell you much about it if I wanted to."

"What about Nimicus?" she asked.

"He's… *different.* Nimicus is something like that, but he wants me to know."

Taunauk added, "It wants you to be afraid."

Shawn smirked grimly. "Yeah, that's pretty much it."

"You should be thankful?"

Shawn turned toward the Endroggen. "And why is that?"

Taunauk shrugged. "Nimicus can't get you in here."

"You know, you used to be better at making people feel better. Where's the wisdom or advice?"

"It is the truth of the moment."

Shawn moved to speak, but no protest escaped.

Helesys smiled. Of course, Taunauk was right. There was nothing they could do about Nimicus at the moment. First, they had to escape. Then they would help Shawn and take on an evil god of dreams.

~

Silence fell between them as the heroes pressed deeper into the gloom. And then cackles and shrieks rang out from beyond the light. Whatever made the sounds seemed to bubble and flow, coming from the left, suddenly from behind, then from the front.

Then came writhing at the edge of the light. A mass of serpents darted in and out of view, undulating and moving around the heroes. Helesys, Taunauk, and Shawn turned their backs to one another and watched. Waited.

Their skin was caked with ash that fell away, revealing oily skin beneath. The ends of the serpents opened into something akin to mouths, split into four jaws, and lined with uncountable rows of thin teeth. But as Helesys opened her magic sense, she could feel nothing akin to a mind. They functioned like a single entity—impossible to tell where one began and another ended.

They were simple things—made-things, in a sense.

The snakes began to churn, growing even more agitated and desperate. They were hungry.

The serpents rose around them, swelling like cackling waves. They churned, back and forth—kept at bay by the *warding light*.

Over her shoulder, Shawn whispered, "I know you have mixed feelings about your wand, but I'm partial to it. So… what do we do?"

"Taunauk?"

Beside her, golden embers flared from Taunauk's face and shoulders. "I can't control my power yet."

Helesys kindled power, eyeing the writhing, hungry masses. Of all the creatures and creations she had felt, these were the simplest of made-things. Even Amadeus's stone-men and One-Mind's mechanical spiders had more *essence*.

She reached out her power, and the magekiller token burned in her metal arm. She could easily match a veteran mage's attacks and dispel their magics… What could she do against these?

"*Restu sonmova, anguillae.*" At her command, the serpents froze.

Just two realms ago, she'd turned the rat-men against one another, and before that she'd controlled the manta ray at the foot of the Godpeak.

Helesys focused her might and her will. In the shared mind-space of the holding spell, she towered over the mass of serpents—growing until they were nothing more than a tiny ball. A pinprick beneath her. She loomed like a titan.

And the old word came to her. "*Mortem.*"

The churning wall of serpents reeled from the light, their shrieks choked off in an instant. They fell, and crumbled into ash. Dead.

Helesys braced herself for the psychic recoil, fearing that she would black out again.

Instead, she felt nothing. Nothing.

Shawn glanced from her to the now barren field. "...You can *do that?*"

"I didn't know," she said, quietly. Helesys looked at her gauntlet. The warding light dimmed enough for her to see the harsh angles of the metal, the points of her fingers. Helesys couldn't see the wand beneath, and doubted she would ever know the depths of its power—her power.

Taunauk asked, "Are you alright?" Worry was wrought across his face.

She nodded. "I'm fine."

Both her comrades lingered a moment, as if they didn't believe her. But after a few moments, they reluctantly turned. The three of them walked together deeper into the gloom.

Shawn asked, "Can you do that to Terrans?"

Helesys glanced at him, but Shawn wouldn't meet her eyes. "I don't think so," she replied in earnest. "They were made-things—simple things. They had no will of their own."

Helesys didn't want to dwell on what she'd done, but she couldn't help it. It had been a despicable thing to take control over another—she'd felt as much when she'd controlled the manta ray. But this... To snuff out the life of another should've pained. Even if the serpents were not truly alive, it should not feel so easy.

She was a soldier, and so battle was in her blood. But even though she'd slain dozens—hundreds—of enemies across the realms, even though some deaths had come easy, it had not been without purpose, effort, or suffering. Using her powers to their full potential left her weak and even pained her.

Perhaps that was why the *death* spell distressed her: It should not feel so meaningless to take the life of another.

Yet they walked through realms of suffering, and now trekked across a monument to death, toward the heart of it all.

Perhaps there was psychic recoil to the spell… for in those moments, Helesys felt like a monster.

Deeper into the gloom.

She only hoped that at the end of it lay absolution.

~ ~ ~

The Ashen Sea

They walked for miles before they reached the end of land. They stood on the cape and looked out across a churning sea of ash. High above, the sky writhed. Helesys thought she caught the salt scent of an ocean, but it was so quick and faint that it might've been a dream.

Fitting—that death and dreams should be so close together.

Helesys stepped to the edge of the land and again dipped her spear beneath the surface. Again, she felt no bottom and found no end to the black depths.

She kept her *warding light*, and cast the *water walk* spell on the three of them. Her power and her attention were taxed by holding both spells, but she had other means: The Gar of Shéslang and the Ring of Winter. They would have to do.

Helesys stepped out onto the ashen sea. Taunauk followed. Shawn stayed on the shore, uncertainty clinging to his face.

"Are you alright, Shawn?" she asked.

He nodded slowly. "I am. I mean, I will be. I can fly. You guys can't. Are you sure about this?"

Helesys patted the jade lemur in her pocket. "We have the lemur if we need it." It wouldn't carry them far, but it would save them in a pinch.

Shawn looked to Taunauk. "What about you, big guy?"

"This is our path. I trust Helesys to keep us afloat."

"It's not that…" Shawn prodded the water with the toe of his boot, then stepped out hesitantly. He stepped quickly toward them.

Helesys asked, "What is it then?"

"Shall we?" Shawn asked, ushering them forward and ignoring the question. Helesys and Taunauk followed.

"Shawn, what is it?" she asked again.

He sighed. "I don't know. Well… No, I don't know. Sometimes this place reminds me of Nimicus—the same ancient, unknowable evil kind of vibes. But I think it's the possibility of dying."

"Dying?"

"No… Dying I can deal with. Especially here. We just get reborn. I mean, the lingering deaths. Especially in these realms. Something about being close to the center—gives me the willies. Regular death is one thing…"

Silence fell between them. Helesys nearly asked more, but saw that Shawn was struggling with the words.

"It's the dreams," Shawn finally said. "The lingering dead don't dream."

~

The heroes walked out across the ashen sea. In moments, the black shore was gone from view. The ash beneath them shimmered like oil, though the *water walk* spell kept them from sinking or slipping. At first, their path was easy.

But the ashen sea grew rougher the further they walked from the cape. Soon, the inky black rolled beneath their feet—growing to hills that crested above their heads.

It was only at the crests that they could see further than a few dozen feet in front of them. In the distance, the rolling sea stretched on.

Slender shapes passed through the waves like sharks, casting matte shadows on the surface. Where the sharks passed the water grew still and calm in their wake before churning again. Helesys followed these outlines, power kindled. Waiting.

The first shark came toward them. It broke the surface, yawning far wider than should've been possible—its mouth lined with axeblade teeth.

Helesys fired her gauntlet. Purple fire tore through half the creature's face, but still its maw lunged toward them.

Helesys and Shawn leapt to the side. Taunauk flared power and cleaved through the beast. The two halves fell beneath the waves, glowing golden before disappearing completely.

Bellows came from all around them, as if the sea itself was boiling. Five more sharks set upon them.

Helesys reached out with her power, but ceased almost immediately—these weren't the simple made things of the serpents on the shore. A *holding* spell might work, but not her *death* spell, and she couldn't risk splitting her power so many ways. Not now.

Helesys ran up the side of the oncoming wave and leapt, momentum carrying her high above the fray. Two sharks passed beneath her, teeth bared, before disappearing. Taunauk and Shawn stayed in the trough—Taunauk conjuring three brightly glowing warriors and cutting through a shark, while Shawn darted between them, eviscerating a second. Helesys fell from the air, blasting thrice more during her fall, bursting the hide of another. She landed and rolled through the frenzy, readying herself.

But the sharks that were not killed outright ignored their injuries. They turned with mangled jaws and bodies—losing no speed.

Shawn slipped an emerald dagger from his coat, its blade glowing softly. The next creature he slashed began to glow with a poisonous green. Moments later, it shuddered and disappeared beneath the surface.

Helesys adjusted her power, turning her power to short spreadblasts. She drew on the Gar of Shéslang to make up for the power draw of the other two spells, and put her back to her comrades.

A shark came for her, rising from the inky water, mouth yawning to reveal vicious teeth. Wide enough to swallow her whole.

Helesys fired, and a flare of purple blotted out the creature. When it faded, chunks of flesh splashed into the water—the top half of the shark blown clean off.

"Messy," Shawn said, as he dodged behind her. Another shark sunk into the water beside her—glowing green and dissolving.

The frenzy grew, sharks setting upon them from all sides—bursting from the troughs and plunging down on them from the crests. They were surrounded by black silhouettes, teeth shining in the alien light of the sky.

But the heroes didn't slow. Didn't falter.

Creatures of shadow were cleaved, broken, or burst by the weapons of the Chosen. They were honed by more than a dozen realms, and thrice as many battles—not counting their lives before imprisonment. They'd been born in darkness, honed by battle, and driven by fate.

The weapon. The vessel. The wisp.

And when it was over, there was nothing to mark the carnage. Dark flesh, inky blood—all sunk beneath the surface. Leaving the heroes standing alone on the ashen sea.

~

A bellow shook the realm—so loud that Helesys winced and even the waves seemed weakened by it. Over the sullen crests, a gargantuan silhouette appeared. A serpent that reached all the way from the waves and into the sky. Its hide was scarred with spiderweb-like cracks that leaked ichor.

Its massive head turned and it lumbered toward the heroes.

"Is that thing as strong as it looks?" Shawn whispered.

Even from so far away, the creature radiated menace. Helesys didn't have to open her magic sense to tell that it was a descendant of the sharks they'd just fought or perhaps a mother come to avenge her young.

Helesys grit her teeth. "It will be hard to kill."

Beside her, Taunauk was smiling. "Attack together, and with overwhelming force."

"Why does he sound excited?" Shawn asked.

"A fitting test before the Wolf King!" Taunauk took off running, golden smoke rolling off his shoulders. He reached the crest of the wave and leapt with superhuman strength, soaring through the air.

Helesys kindled strength and sprinted after him. Shawn was right behind her, tugging at the wraps of his forearms.

Helesys's vision flashed back to their very first realm—the flooded temple where they fought the fishmen and the hydra. The image of Taunauk disappearing into one of its mouths. *Their first death.*

The serpent bellowed, its face splitting into a dozen jaws full of glistening teeth—so wide it looked as if the void had opened up into a dappled night sky. Taunauk hung in the air like a north star.

Then he roared and swung his axe. Golden light streaked across the sky nearly as long as the serpent, cutting a giant's stroke—his ancestor's power flowing through the blade. The titan bellowed and reeled as a length of its face slid away—like the sky itself had been split. Taunauk sailed past, his leap carrying him somewhere behind the serpent's twisting girth.

Shawn sprinted ahead, skin and clothes turning to mist, unleashing his hidden power—half running, half gliding over the waves. Even with Helesys's bolstered speed, she couldn't keep up. Shawn was already waves ahead, and a breath later he was running up the flank of the angry beast. Green wounds hemorrhaged in his wake.

No matter how the serpent writhed, it couldn't shake him. The wounds spread—but too few!

The serpent's mouth closed and it dove headlong into the sea—

Toward Helesys.

Her eyes went wide as the beast grew in her vision, like a wall were falling on her.

She compounded her strength with the spear, ran up the next crest, and leapt. She soared out of the way as the serpent plunged into the sea. The crash was deafening, as if the world exploded behind her. Helesys sprawled across the waves, and then was thrown again as more were kicked up in the serpent's wake. By the time she came to a stop, the last segments of the tail plunged into the water.

She fought to stand on the rolling surf. Forced herself to breathe slowly.

"Helesys!" Shawn called.

"Stay quiet!" She could *feel* both of her allies walking, some-where beyond the rolling surf. But she also sensed danger below.

It was coming back.

For a moment, Helesys had wondered which of them the serpent would be drawn to. Taunauk's spirits, Shawn's dreams, or her magic.

She needn't wonder.

Helesys leapt as high as she could—the Gar of Shéslang amplifying her strength. She soared upward, and the water ex-ploded beneath her. The serpent chased her, maw open wide. Before her momentum was lost, Helesys twisted and aimed her metal arm down at the beast.

She could only split her power so many ways—she kept *water walk* and let go the *warding light*. The world plunged into near-absolute darkness—spared only by the twisting purple clouds above, and the glint of their light playing across the ser-pent's teeth below.

Helesys relaxed her strength, keeping only enough for the task. The rest of her power went to her gauntlet and was com-pounded by the spear that had pierced a god.

She screamed and fired repeatedly. Purple destruction rained down on the serpent, illuminating it in flashes—shatter-ing teeth and punching holes through its face. Each blast catapulted Helesys higher and higher into the darkness, wrenching her shoulder so hard it felt like her metal arm would tear free. The serpent roared, the sound rattling her teeth. It climbed into the sky, spiraling after her in desperation.

In between the flashes of purple power, there were the faintest sparks of green—then a single blinding flash of gold.

The serpent stopped, but Helesys kept firing—kept firing until the enormous maw listed and began to fall away. Gold flashed three more times, and in the light, Helesys saw the titanic serpent cut clean through.

Breath caught in her throat, and Helesys fell. Far below, the chunks of titanic serpent crashed into the water, sending the ashen sea into a maelstrom. She turned all of her power toward her strength and toward maintaining the *water walk* spell.

Helesys landed high on the crest of a wave, then tumbled down the side of it. But the ashen sea buckled like it were in the throes of an earthquake, and she was thrown again—impacting the side of another wave as if it were solid rock. She gasped in the darkness as the waves hurled her twice more. She clung to the spear.

What felt like minutes later, the waves finally lost their rage, and Helesys stood atop them—battered, but alive. She relaxed her strength slowly, so that she didn't lose her footing, then conjured her *warding light*. The darkness receded, revealing an empty and spent landscape.

Helesys waited, afraid to call out. But she felt them. Moments later, Taunauk and Shawn strode out of the darkness wearing looks of stoic pride.

The three stood together in silent triumph as the waves died.

~ ~ ~

Grave Dunes

Some hour later, the waves grew to their normal roll. The heroes jogged on, led by the *warding light*. Meanwhile, the sky continued churning overhead.

When Helesys was certain that they walked alone, and that no more monsters stalked them in the dark, she finally spoke.

"That was most impressive," she said to Taunauk.

Shawn added, "When are you going to teach us those tricks?"

Beside her, the Endroggen still emanated golden mist. The excitement of battle had left him, as did his earlier mirth. Now he stared off across the waves, eyes glowing.

"An Endroggen army brought to bear. A force never known by the living nor the dead."

But his voice was not his own. It was the voice of his father speaking through his lips.

Helesys slowed and grasped Taunauk's arm, halting him. "Rehkoros, where is Taunauk?" *Where is my friend?*

"My son has not left you," the weathered voice said. The golden mist grew denser from Taunauk's shoulders. "But channeling the strength of so many has left him drained. So for now, I walk with you, and share the burden with him."

Shawn asked, "He'll be alright, right?"

"In time." Rehkoros gestured for them to follow, and as he did, Helesys swore she could see the father's figure superimposed over Taunauk's body.

They walked, and Helesys's curiosity grew.

"Taunauk told us you had talked to each other about his childhood. That you were mending things…"

Rehkoros grumbled. "I know your question."

"Taunauk means a lot to us," she said plainly.

Rehkoros eyed her and smiled meekly. "You could've been born Endroggen. Civilized Terrans choose their words carefully. We do not.

"It is not a simple thing to mend the past. I have talked more with my son than I did in all my living years… Perhaps if we had more time, things could be different, but we're close to the end." Rehkoros shook his head. "One day, my son will join me in Accaelum."

Rehkoros looked at Helesys again. "Do you think that someone can ever truly change? Become someone else?"

Even behind the golden glow, Helesys saw the emotion welling in the father's eyes. Was he asking about Taunauk, or about himself?

Did it matter?

"Yes," she finally said. "I think they can, but they have to want to, desperately. When I died on the battlefield and was reborn, I wasn't whole. I was nothing but pain and anger. Just emotion. Since waking here, I've remade myself. I'm no longer ruled by my emotions. No longer just a weapon. I feel whole again, even if it took a wand to do so.

"But it took me losing everything to do it, even losing my memories. Forgetting who I was. Making peace with it, I suppose."

Helesys looked to Shawn, waiting for his input, but the rogue didn't meet her eye. He would have insight too—a being who lived as both a god and a Terran...

When Shawn didn't answer, Helesys continued. "Taunauk is the same. Whatever he was before, he is no longer just the Vessel of his people. He has bonded with us. After we escape, Taunauk will change, and be a new man..." She looked at the father. "If he can change, so can you."

They continued walking in silence, and it was a long moment before Rehkoros spoke.

"Thank you." A moment later, he smirked. "Of all the other Terrans I met in life, you will be the one to learn Endroggen blood magic."

She asked, "Why do you say that?"

"A feeling. You claimed that when you died, you were little more than pain and raw emotion. You're more in tune with such things than any of my people. The elders spend their entire lives meditating and pouring through memories to achieve that understanding. When you claim our blood magic, you will truly be a force unlike any other. If there is anyone who can help you learn, it is Taunauk."

Rehkoros spoke the words with a father's pride—not just of Taunauk, but of her as well. Hope swelled within her, not just for escape but for what she might become—that there was something *after* escape.

Silence lingered. So did peace.

Shawn asked, "Helesys, didn't you get your spear from something like that snake?"

Shéslang, the god-serpent from the forgotten city. She thought back to the immense cavern that stretched on for miles. How it spoke of rampaging and boring through solid rock in moments.

Helesys smiled. "This snake wasn't *that* big. Shéslang was much bigger."

~

Time stretched on, and in the distorted realm, Helesys truly had no idea how much time was passing, or if such a concept even held sway anymore.

The rolling waves gave way to dunes that glinted like gemstones in the *warding light*. Rather than sand, they seemed to be made of glass worn smooth by wear, like each was a stone on the edge of a pond. They grew larger and more numerous until their edges joined together, forming a solid shoreline.

Helesys dimmed her light until it was only a candle. A plane of shimmering, rolling glass stretched out to the horizon. Light from the chaotic sky played purple across it. The faintest smell of salt and sweat hung on dead air.

They stood on the shoreline, staring across the sprawl. The heroes looked to each other before continuing in silence.

Shapes began to appear, half-submerged in the glass. They flickered in and out of sight like the images from the prior realm beside the river of glass. But these shapes defied explanation—even when Helesys forced herself to look, forced her magic sight to pry into the realm, the shapes were little more than shadow. Little more than abstract silhouettes.

One might've been a bat, another a feather as tall as a tower. Another looked like a long and slender crab. One that might've been a spider's long legs or the sickles of a single hand. So many more defied description.

Shawn reached out to one that might've been a rose or a face screaming in pain. His fingers lingered just over the surface. "Those shadow beings we keep seeing… These are their corpses. I guess even they die after being trapped here long enough."

"No," Taunauk said in his own voice, staring at something distant. A shadow that Helesys couldn't see. "It is another lingering death for them."

"Now you're just mincing words," Shawn replied. "What is death or a lingering death to something that cannot *truly* die?"

Helesys shook her head. It was too much to contemplate. "For once, I'm glad to be mortal."

Taunauk said, "I agree."

~

The heroes stalked deeper across the landscape of marbled glass. Bulbous outcroppings began to appear, like solid, half-formed bubbles. Soon they were so large and numerous that the heroes walked between them, pausing at clearings to clamber up the side and scout ahead.

The sky above was thick with purple clouds, like a rolling sea—growing ever more violent.

Taunauk's glow had receded, and he spoke for himself once again. "Danger approaches. *We* can feel it."

Shawn stood atop one of the large boulders and called down, "There's nothing out there, Taunauk. Absolutely noth—"

The sky split, and a dark meteor fell to the ground. The glass beneath them trembled, and somewhere far below,

Helesys heard cracks as if the realm itself had split. Something in the clouds growled like rolling thunder.

Across the realm, smoke rose from the meteor—

Then it stood.

A bristling thing of shadow. A dragon out of nightmares. Even from so far away, it towered over the landscape, its skin featureless and void-black. It stood like a bat, wings stretching across its forelimbs and hind limbs. Instead of spines, wriggling serpents protruded from every angle.

Three heads appeared, emerging from the shadow one at a time as if jostling for control of the body. A thick dragon's head with wide-set horns, another like a slim-snouted crocodile. The last was a short snout with overhanging fangs. It roared up at the sky in three voices at once—a bellow, a cackle, and a trill.

Lightning erupted from the sky, the bolts dancing across the landscape. The ground exploded everywhere a bolt touched down, sending glass flying across the realm.

Shawn leapt down, and the heroes took cover behind one of the boulders. Helesys kindled strength. Shawn screamed something, but she couldn't hear him over the maelstrom. Just around the boulder, Helesys saw lightning coursing toward the sky in retaliation.

They huddled before a battle of dragons—of titans—while the world rumbled and glass shards rained down on them.

Then the boulder in front of them exploded.

Helesys was flung backward, slamming into other mounds over glass and rolling across the ground. Her eyes rang and her vision wavered. Her shoulder and knee ached sharply—as if glass had been ground into them.

Helesys pushed herself up and stumbled toward a boulder. Leaned on it for support. It felt as if minutes passed, but Helesys knew it could only have been moments.

She looked through her hazy vision for Taunauk and Shawn, but found neither.

Then she looked for the dragon—

Found it standing still, its battle paused.

Looking right at her.

Helesys summoned more power, but found her spear silent—gone. She whirled around, looking frantically for it. She found nothing but mounds of shattered glass.

The dragon trilled, calling her attention back. The short-snouted face spasmed, and then black oozed sprayed through its overlapping fangs. The torrent sailed across the landscape—drops landing around Helesys.

Each black spot grew long and thick, the end of it splitting into four jaws, full of thin teeth—*the serpents from the dunes.* Hundreds of the creatures slithered toward her, clumping into waves. Helesys kindled her warding light to keep the mass of creatures at bay.

She reached out with her power. This time, she didn't bother holding the simple creatures. In the mindspace, she towered over them like a titan, and she brushed them away with a word.

"Mortem." All around, snakes crumbled into ash, and Helesys felt nothing.

The dragon trilled again, its face turning sideways in confusion.

Helesys reached out again with her power, this time for the dragon, but the world didn't fall away—

~

It felt as if she'd been dropped into an ocean. Deep, cold, dark. Endless. Like Helesys was treading water and looking down at an abyss of a creature.

A mortal staring into the mind of something far older than she could comprehend. Far older than Movernus, the god that made her world.

Beneath her, the ocean blinked.

Frigid black waves rolled over her, tasting like bile.

Helesys dredged power from her wand—all that she could—and felt herself swell against the tide. But she didn't have the Gar of Shéslang, the relic that had pierced the god-serpent and had helped her face so many other foes far beyond her power. She was no match without it.

She was alone. Without even the comforting voice of her wand.

Her heart thrummed with fear and with anger. It felt like she was back on the Eternal Battlefield. Alone and dying.

But Helesys had survived then. She'd been remade and given a second chance. No—that wasn't quite right. She'd been *rebuilt*—that had been Aradi's doing.

Helesys *remade herself.* At one point she might've been a wand, or fear, anger, and raw remotion—nothing but the bone and sinew of a mind. Now she was something else—something more—

But she *remembered.*

Helesys focused on that old pain of her death and rebirth. She drew on her anger, the fear, the confusion, and desperation. *Her Rage.*

And power swelled within her. Emotion in her chest, and magic in her arm—emotion compounding her arcane might.

In the dark ocean of the mindspace, Helesys grew. Soon she was the size of a whale and then an island. She swelled with power until she was no longer treading water, no longer look-ing down at an unknowable abyss.

Now the black dragon stood before her, simmering with shadow. It still towered over her in the mindspace—easily ten times her height—but Helesys stood definitely, hands clenched and shaking.

All three heads of the dragon turned curiously, and the thin crocodile face recoiled. For a moment, Helesys glimpsed into its mind—almost knew its name. The word was so alien that her wand couldn't translate it and she couldn't pronounce—something akin to a force of nature.

The dragon was used to towering over lesser creatures, trampling them. Devouring. Destroying. It was used to staring its own brethren in the eye—not some lesser creature. An in-sect.

How dare she challenge it.

Now it had forgotten all its brethren and mortal enemy in the sky. All three heads focused on Helesys.

The dragon's head with wide-set horns bellowed, its voice shaking the mindscape. Lightning crackled in its maw—an an-swer to Helesys's challenge.

~

The mindscape fell away, and once more Helesys was standing on the landscape of glass. Across the rubble, the black dragon conjured lightning—mouth wide, eyes closed.

Helesys funneled all her magic to her strength and ran. Her legs pounded, and her feet crunched on rubble. She hurdled boulders.

She dove behind the largest ball of glass just as lightning erupted. The world flashed white. Bolts of electricity lashed like bullwhips around the landscape. Glass exploded every-where they touched, turning the realm into a maelstrom.

It was over one terrible moment later.

Helesys shunted power to her gauntlet, leaving just enough strength in her to keep from breaking her own arm. She rose and aimed her gauntlet at the dragon. Its heads writhed, jock-eying for control of the body.

Purple blasts erupted from her arm, rattling the metal in her shoulder. The first shots slammed into it, sending ripples of black and purple across its body.

The dragon turned back toward her, the two heads yielding to the one that conjured lightning.

Helesys grimaced at the pain and searched again for her Rage. The power that had come so easily a moment ago now eluded her when she needed it most. There was only a faint taste of *anger*—but it was enough.

Again and again, she fired—now each blast pushed the weaver back, her feet sliding across the broken glass. Each blast slammed into the dragon, and it recoiled backward.

Helesys stumbled. She caught herself, but so had the dragon. It stared at her, conjuring lightning again.

"Helesys!" She turned to see Shawn beside her, handing her the spear. "You dropped this," he said.

She smirked and took the spear. "Thanks."

"Would've been here sooner but—"

Bolts of lightning whipped across the landscape again, and the pair ducked behind a boulder. Helesys breathed deep—that blast felt weaker than before.

"As I was saying," the rogue said, brushing himself off, "I would've been here sooner, but that lightning is tough to avoid. Besides, I was waiting on—"

The world flashed golden, as if the realm had been cut in two. The dragon reeled from Taunauk's empowered slash, then roared, shaking glass all across the realm.

Helesys could barely see the Endroggen across the battlefield. He stood at the foot of the dragon, like a mouse against a bear, and with each strike, arcs of light a hundred feet tall sprang from his axe.

But as Taunauk slashed, the dragon dodged. Its bulk became formless as it lurched out of the way, like it were stuffed inside a cocoon of shadow—in between each, its body reformed to bite at Taunauk. So, barbarian and dragon became locked in a deadly waltz.

Beside her, Shawn pulled a rapier from his ethereal pocket. A simple silver blade with an ornate guard around the handle—Helesys looked twice at the absurdity of the long sword coming from nowhere.

"Forgot I had that," Shawn said. With his other hand, he tugged at the wrappings around his wrist and ghostly mist rose from his body. Then he sprinted toward the dragon—moving in a blink.

The dragon spewed snakes across the battlefield. Taunauk's axeswings cut through dozens as they flew through the air, but hundreds more landed all around. Helesys reached out with her power and culled them with a *word*. All around, serpents burst into ash.

In the same moment, Shawn climbed the back of the dragon in a blur of gray. He plunged the length of the sword into the creature and its body rippled. Cracks of purple appeared in its shadow form. Screeches rang out as the creature recoiled from Shawn and shifted to avoid Taunauk's attacks.

Helesys had the Gar of Shéslang now, but she couldn't fire at the dragon without risking hitting Shawn. Nor could she hold the creature, even with the spear. But she could slow it.

Helesys amplified her might with the spear. *"Lente et gravis."*

She lurched forward and struggled to keep her footing. All the other times she'd used the spell, it had been a simple thing—not even with the contested mindspace of the *holding* spell. But slowing the dragon was another thing entirely—she felt as if her spear were tethered to it and she was holding the reins. Finally, she kindled strength and grasped the spear with both hands.

The dragon roared. With the spell *slowing* it, each of Taunauk's thunderous strikes landed, cleaving deep into its shadowy form, which grew all the more fragmented and purple as Shawn assaulted with his sword.

Helesys smirked with satisfaction. For a moment, their victory over a god seemed sure.

The dragon pulsed, its form stretching nearly twice its normal size—the ends flaring into spiderwebs of darkness. It recoiled backward, and when its head emerged again, lightning crackled in its mouth.

Taunauk and Shawn had no time to move. Images of destruction flashed before her eyes. Death.

Instead of ducking for cover, Helesys leapt atop the nearest boulder of glass. Words of power had come to her unbidden from the wand—from her direct connection—and now they came again. She grasped the Gar of Shéslang with elven and metal hands and leveled it at the dragon.

"Omnis potentia veni ad me!" And as she screamed, her words were blotted out by the full force of the dragon's lightning—a realm's worth of stormclouds bottled and unleashed in an instant. Destructive power arced toward her, lashing across the

battlefield and scarring ravines into the landscape. The world trembled.

Taunauk's gold and Shawn's silver were blotted out.

Helesys focused all her willpower into the spell, and as the lightning stretched across the battlefield, it coalesced on Helesys. The wild arcs of lightning leapt to her spear, and the metal grew white hot. She held on tight, letting power seep into her strength—

But she couldn't contain such power. As each bolt leapt to her spear, her hold on the spells—*coalescence* and *strength*—grew more tenuous. The spear grew bright as a star, and the world was awash in the smell of ozone, molten glass, and Helesys's own burning flesh.

Power coursed violently through her, spear to metal hand, through her body and back again. She could feel it slowing within her, building up heat, burning her alive—

The Rage that had come to her so easily in darkness eluded her, and she didn't have time to contemplate it. Helesys felt the limits of her power, like a dam about to crumble before a storm.

Instead of holding it, she let the power flow through her, letting the speed of it build. And in that perilous moment, a part of her was at peace and would've smiled, for she *knew the feeling*—it was the same as when she first called on the power of her metal arm and the wand within: The dredging of power and holding it while it compounded.

In moments, lightning was sucked from the landscape, and lived within her—built so ferociously that it arced off Helesys in mad, desperate bursts, begging to be unleashed.

So much power sparked from her that Helesys could barely see the dragon across from her. And she said a silent prayer to Movernus that Taunauk and Shawn were out of the way.

Helesys screamed, and a single, massive bolt of lightning erupted from the spear.

The world went white and silent, and Helesys was flung backward, hurtling across the glass, and slammed into another boulder.

Dazed, Helesys bolstered her strength. Her vision relaxed from blinding white to a haze. Deafness became ringing in her ears. Helesys pushed herself up. Even with kindled strength, her arms shook so violently she had to lean against the boulder.

Across the battlefield, what had once been the dragon looked like a mountain of darkness cracked in half. The edges of it wavered, and feeble cries sounded across the realm.

Helesys breathed deep. In her metal hand, she held tight to the Gar of Shéslang—the metal of both smoldered with steam, but were otherwise unharmed. She still couldn't stand up, but her strength would return.

She'd done it. She'd held more power than a mortal had any right to—turned a god's own power back at it. She felt a spark of pride as she looked aT the dragon's corpse.

Helesys tried to call for Taunauk, but pain wracked her chest, and she doubled over. *"Stercus,"* she whispered. Elven hand clutching her chest and leaning on her spear, Helesys forced herself to stand tall—to look for her friends.

Then wings of shadow stretched out, like black spiderwebs reaching up to the sky, and the dragon leapt into the clouds. Somewhere high above, an old god—a still living god—roared.

~ ~ ~

The Scar

Taunauk and Shawn ran across the landscape toward Helesys. Her pain lifted, if only a little, at the sight of them.

Shawn ran all the way up to her, stopped suddenly, and grasped her shoulders. She winced, and he relented, then looked Helesys over. "Your hands—your face… Tamir's beard. What did you do?"

Taunauk stood beside him, possessed with a golden glow. His eyes twitched, and though his pupils were hidden behind the light, she knew he was assessing her injuries.

"I'll manage," she said, though now she realized her injuries were worse than she thought: Her metal hand steamed, and her elven hand was blistered and bleeding, and the skin across her arm, shoulders, and neck was the same. But she was already healing from her bolstered strength. She smirked, and added, "It will leave scars."

Shawn chuckled. "Better than that bastard dragon got off with. That was a beautiful shot."

Helesys gestured to his vest and cloak. "I think between the two of us, you got the better power." The rogue was completely unscathed. Not even covered in dust.

"It's not without its own problems," he replied sheepishly. "I let loose too much or too often and I'm liable to fly away on you again."

They both looked at Taunauk, who stood glowing and silent.

Helesys asked, "Are you there, Taunauk?"

A dozen voices answered, *"He is with you, weaver, but he is resting."*

"Rehkoros?" she asked.

"He comforts his son."

Helesys nodded. She supposed all power had its price, though she was not fond of Taunauk losing himself so. Still, there was comfort that his father and the other Endroggen were with him. Rehkoros would keep him safe.

"Come," Helesys said, resting her elven hand on his shoulder. "I grow weary of this realm."

~

They walked wearily across the dunes of glass while purple clouds rolled above. Helesys felt the seam of the realm growing closer.

"Only a few more miles," she said. Which was good because their battle with the dragon had left her weak. Every muscle burned and her bones felt as if they ground against one another when she moved. Even the struts and wires in her metal arm ached. She could've kindled strength, but she tried to reserve her power. Who knew what other horrors lay in the center of the realm.

There was a part of her that took solace in the pain—relished it, even. There was a price to power, to victory, and Helesys would pay it. To numb the pain and push it aside would only prolong the debt. The only way to push herself to her limits was to know the cost.

Besides, pain was preferable to numbness. And emptiness. She couldn't help but dwell on the hollow feeling when she destroyed the serpents with a word. It had been too easy. Too simple. No—the pain was better. It made her feel real and whole—like a Terran, not a weapon.

They walked in silence—not only because Helesys was weary, but because Taunauk's body glowed with possession and Shawn seemed far off in thought.

And because the black dragon still bellowed in the sky. It hadn't emerged from the clouds, but Helesys knew it was following them.

Soon, they came to a ridge and stopped at the edge of it. A cliff extended out to the horizon in either direction, and dropped hundreds of feet, maybe even a thousand feet down… But as Helesys extended her magic perception, she realized that it was not a cliff. The edge curved around, forming a circle hundreds of miles across. The surface was powdered glass, weathered by deep time.

And across swathes of it, there were scrapes and gouges as deep as canyons. One was visible by eye just at the edge of the horizon, and in that spot looked as if the world had collapsed into shadow. Helesys followed the other gorges in her mind. Some were larger than others, and they converged somewhere in the center of the crater—as if something vast and incomprehensible had tried a dozen times to claw its way out.

Whatever *thing* had been responsible was long gone, and Helesys thanked Movernus for that because they would pass through one of the smaller gorges on the way to the center.

"It's a crater," she said. "A scar in the realm. Whatever made it is gone."

Of her companions, Shawn chuckled uneasily.

Helesys added, "This is as good a place as any to rest." She sat a few feet from the cliffside, and the others sat beside her.

Helesys reached for her pack out of habit, but realized she wasn't hungry. She offered it to Taunauk and Shawn, but they refused.

"It's the realm," Shawn said, still misty. "The closer we get to the center, the closer we get to the Wolf King, the more the illusions break down. Hence, why we don't need to eat."

Helesys slipped her pack back over her shoulder. "The dream realm is like that?"

"Yes. It's like… Well, it's like being in a dream." He smiled sheepishly.

Helesys asked, "What about your sword? Is that from the dream realm, too?"

Shawn reached into his pocket and pulled the rapier out. It was a comical motion again, seeing the absurdly long blade come from nowhere. It gleamed in the strange light of the realm.

Shawn looked it over like he was half-remembering it. "It's called *Mother's Tears*. Whatever power an enemy uses—doesn't matter what—this severs their connection to it. Could be their physical strength, their magic, even something like rage, I think. …I don't remember where I got it." He chuckled. "Still works."

Their eyes fell to Taunauk, who sat, glowing, and looking out over the crater.

Helesys said, "It took Taunauk many realms to regain his memories. Do all the Endroggen remember their lives before?"

"We remember. I remember—" but as they spoke, the voices grew discordant. A hundred voices overlapping and recounting stories. Helesys couldn't understand any one of them. After a few moments, the voices trailed off, as if they realized the hopelessness of it.

"One at a time," Shawn joked. Taunauk turned toward him, mouth opening hesitantly. "I was joking," the rogue added.

~

Respite was short-lived, and the heroes descended the precarious slope of the crater. It wasn't a sheer cliff, but it was steep enough all three heroes had to climb at first rather than slide down. After what felt like an hour of climbing, the slope leveled off enough for them to shuffle carefully down.

Helesys said, "It's much deeper than I thought at first."

"How far to the center?" Taunauk asked, voices overlapping his own.

"A hundred miles, at least."

"It won't be that far," Shawn replied.

Helesys asked, "What do you mean?"

"It's like a dream. We won't experience the walk the same way we would if we were *actually* walking that distance. Trust me."

A roar echoed through the sky above. It rattled the cliffside and sent fine shards of glass sliding down the slope.

"Which is a good thing!" Shawn added. "Let's get out of here."

~

The heroes moved faster, sliding down the side of the crater. And when they could, they started running, tearing across the landscape with bolstered speed.

All the while, the dragon followed, screeching at them from the clouds. They dared not slow.

It felt like only minutes had passed, but one of the dark scars that marked the center of the realm lay ahead—just at the edge of the horizon.

The dragon's calls grew furious, and moments later, gigantic spiderweb-wings flashed across the sky as the dragon dipped below the clouds.

"Stercus," Shawn said as they ran, "He's not looking any worse for wear."

The dragon swooped around, crossing miles in a breath. Lightning crackled in its maw.

Helesys kindled what power she could in her gauntlet, firing blasts as she ran. But the dragon was too far away; even though her blasts traveled as fast as an arrow—faster—the dragon dodged them effortlessly.

The dragon breathed lightning, and nigh-instantaneously, the bolts were upon them. Electricity lashed violently across the crater like hundreds of whips, blasting chunks of glass into the air.

The heroes ran ever faster, dodging left and right. A blast lashed between them—Helesys barely avoiding it. If they could just make it to the wound in the center of the realm then they would have cover. Perhaps they could force the dragon to fight them up close again. But now they were out in the open, and the dragon was content to blast them from afar.

Helesys fired volley after volley of power at the dragon as it passed. Most passed harmlessly, but a few passed close enough that the dragon changed course—lurching like a mass of liquid rather than a creature.

But the dragon fired back too, and as the heroes grew ever nearer to the canyon, the dragon grew more desperate and more ferocious. Lightning crashed around them—

Helesys screamed, *"Omnis potentia veni ad me!"* This time, she only drew enough of the lightning to shield her and the others. Lightning coursed through her, and while Helesys slowed her run so that she could contain, it didn't pain her as before. She released it back at the dragon, and this time the bolt struck true. The dragon lurched and stole back into the clouds.

They were nearly at the foot of the canyon. It cut deep into the realm, and the glass walls glowed a brilliant purple. There was darkness beyond, and Helesys couldn't tell how deep the canyon truly was, but anything was better than out in the open. They slipped into one of the small fissures, following the path as it zig-zagged through the cracked ground. Soon the top of the fissure was above their heads, and the boiling sky was only a sliver.

The dragon roared, and lightning flashed above them, playing across the top of the canyon. Shards of glass blotted out the sky and rained down. The heroes ducked until the blasts stopped, then kept running.

They came to an opening in the fissure and stopped suddenly—Taunauk holding them back. There was a sheer cliff and a hundred foot drop to the next segment of the canyon. Below them, the canyon was impossibly wide and cloaked in darkness that seemed to boil. At once, Helesys was overcome by power. It boiled in the darkness and radiated upward like heat.

She whispered, "Do either of you—"

"Feel something ominous?" Shawn asked. *"Yes.* We need to turn around. Now."

The dragon swooped down in front of them. Its body rippled with shadow—hard lines threaded inside it, like dark lightning. Its wings stretched out in black spiderwebs, reaching hundreds of feet across—so close it nearly blotted out the horizon. It roared, conjuring lightning in its mouth.

Helesys churned power and raised her gauntlet. She only had a moment—

Something enormous reached out of the canyon. At first, Helesys thought it another of the colossal serpents from the ashen sea. No—a hand reached up and seized the black dragon. A hand large enough to wrap completely around it.

The dragon screeched, wings and head thrashing. A crack echoed across the canyon—something between glass and thick tree breaking. Its wings fell limp and began to shrink. Its cry grew meek.

The hand squeezed. The dragon crunched in its grip and hung lifeless—Helesys felt it diminish at the touch of the *thing.* Then the hand released, and the dragon fluttered down into the abyss, turning to smoke and ash as it disappeared into the gloom.

~

Darkness rose from the canyon, like a black tree. Up and up, until it towered over them and blotted out the sky.

A horrid sound echoed across the realm, like whining glass, tearing flesh, and roaring fire—a voice—and it echoed in Helesys's mind as her wand translated.

"MEAT FOR THE TROUGH."

Slowly, it turned toward the heroes. A colossal shadow, vaguely Terran-shaped.

Helesys looked up in horror. She knew—she knew that even though its form was Terran, it couldn't be further from the truth. It wore the form like a performer might wear a mask—

But that wasn't what made her shiver with fear. Somehow, she understood the creature. Somehow, her wand had been able to translate. Which meant the creature's mind—however alien—wasn't too far from their own.

Its face was little more than a silhouette of shadow, but Helesys felt a gaze upon her as it looked down at them.

Then it reached a hand toward them. Shawn screamed. Taunauk roared.

Helesys bolstered strength and spoke in the creature's voice—her words echoing across the canyon. *"We are not meat!"*

It paused, hand hanging in the air.

Shawn muttered, "Helesys, we don't have time for this!"

"We don't need to fight it," she said. "We just need to get around it."

The creature's deafening voice echoed again. *"YOU SPEAK THE DREAD VOICE… BUT YOU ARE NOT MY KIN."* Helesys and the others winced as its voice rose.

"Still have that jade lemur?" Shawn asked.

Helesys patted the tiny statuette in her pocket. "Yes." Then she said, *"We are not your kin. We are travelers. We seek the seam of the realm."*

The creature tilted its head curiously. *"NO ONE ES-CAPES. NOT EVEN ME. NO ONE CAN ESCAPE MY SISTER."*

"The Gatekeeper…" The Queen.

"THAT IS WHAT MEAT CALL HER."

Helesys's eyes fell to the sprawling canyon that stretched out to the horizon—that dwarfed the titan looming above them. The canyon that was one small part of the crater and the wounds within it. The scar that blighted the realm.

"Helesys…" Shawn whispered. "We need to go."

A question bubbled up from deep within her… One that Helesys couldn't stop herself from asking.

"You didn't make this crater, did you?"

"MY SISTER EMERGED HERE."

Images flickered through Helesys's mind, unbidden—*something* vast and incomprehensible that had tried a dozen times to climb from the crater. *Something* that she'd glimpsed and forgotten in the prior realm in the gorge of glass, where ground up souls seeped through and fell into infinite darkness. Something that was too much to see, it could only be felt: *The maw of something vast and incomprehensible eating thousands of broken souls.*

The *Gatekeeper*—the *Queen*—that fed on all imprisoned here.

"Mother of Movernus…" Helesys whispered.

"IT'S ALRIGHT, MEAT," the titan said. *"COME TO ME. ONE TROUGH TO ANOTHER."* It reached out for the heroes.

Taunauk roared in a thousand voices, and blazed with golden light. The air around them grew hot with magic. Taunauk swung his axe, and an arc of power cut a golden fissure in the sky.

The creature shrieked as power cut into it. The whine of glass grew to an agonizing crescendo, and the titan recoiled.

Helesys pulled the jade lemur from her pocket and screamed, *"Messoris umbra, matris' vellus, ventus equitem!."*

The totem shook and leapt from Helesys's grasp, the stone already elongating and forming limbs, fur sprouting from the stone. As if knowing the urgency in her voice, the jade lemur was fully grown in moments, and the heroes leapt on its back a moment later—Helesys, Taunauk, and then Shawn.

"*Volare, pueri,*" Helesys commanded in the old words. *Fly, child.*

The lemur unfurled its wings, and in one powerful motion, it leapt into the air. The same magic that bound it to her command held them fast to its back, but Helesys and the others still held tight to its fur.

They climbed into the air, but the titan recovered, turned toward them, and swiped with a hand that dwarfed them. Taunauk roared again and slashed, axe carving across the sky—the force of it twisting the lemur and causing them to drop.

For a dreadful moment, Helesys's heart was in her throat as they fell. At the back, Shawn gasped. Wings beat frantically as the monster roared behind them. A moment later, the lemur's powerful wings righted them.

Helesys couldn't use her power to shoot or to slow the creature, lest the recoil knock them from the sky. After using the holding spell on the dark dragon, she doubted that even with the Gar of Shéslang she could stop the titan. Instead, she called upon the Ring of Winter and all of its icy power. She had no idea of knowing how violent its new depths would be—the curse of cold fire swelled within it now, desperate to be unleashed. So, Helesys bolstered her strength and split the power of the staff to control the recoil of what she was about to do.

"Murum glaciei tempestatemque," she cried.

A torrent of ice leapt from her ring and flowed down toward the canyon. The titan recovered from Taunauk's attack and stepped toward them, shaking the realm. A wall of ice stretched across the canyon, spreading a hundred feet wide and reaching up until the titan disappeared beneath it—still Helesys poured icy power into it. And in the center she slipped a tinge of the Curse.

The jade lemur beat its wings, sprinting away. They were dangerously low, but spared nothing for altitude as the black landscape rushed beneath them.

A horrid crack echoed through the air.

Shawn shouted, "It's breaking through! It won't hold."

"It doesn't have to," Helesys called back.

Twice more, the titan struck the wall of ice. On the next blow, it shattered, sending chunks of ice flying through the ice.

Again, Helesys called on the *wall of frost*, this time to shield them from debris. She glanced back to see if her ploy worked.

Behind them, cold fire sprung from the destroyed wall and climbed the titan. In moments, it was covered in blue flames. *Cursed.*

It wailed—the sound of heavy bells rung and shattered—so loud, Helesys covered her ears and bolstered strength. Through the turmoil, her wand translated. *"HELP ME, SIS-TER! HELP ME!"* It struck feebly against the remaining sections of wall and then at the edges of the canyon, writhing in pain.

They flew away on the back of the jade lemur, leaving the titan behind in agony.

It wasn't until the burning titan grew small in the distance that they heard a rumble—not thunder, nor anything else in the clouds. Something distant. Something that might not have been in the realm, but rolled like thunder all the same. Helesys felt her wand hum with translation, though there were no words. It was the Queen's answer to the titan's pain—to her kin.

The Queen laughed.

~ ~ ~

The Well

They flew over the canyon, and the scar of void grew beneath them. There was no telling how deep the wound in the realm was, but it grew ever wider beneath them. Despite this, Helesys breathed easy, even as she felt the lemur's strength fading.

"We'll need to stop soon and let our mount rest," she said.

Shawn replied from the back of the lemur, "I could do with one of those, too. Far too much excitement for one day… Gods, how many days has it been?"

Helesys didn't answer. She was worried about the barbarian sitting between them. Taunauk said nothing… and Helesys could only turn enough to see his arms and legs glowing a brilliant gold. Using his power to fend off the titan had left him weakened.

They finally landed on a cliff—one of the joining points of two massive canyons. Past that, the canyons merged with others, forming a sea of darkness.

Helesys and the others dismounted from the lemur, and she called it back to her hand. In moments, the giant lemur had returned to her, back to a tiny stone trinket.

When Helesys and Shawn looked at Taunauk, it was just as she feared. Taunauk glowed brilliantly, his eyes completely glazed over with light and staring back at her absently. Helesys clenched her hand—he'd used far too much power to keep them safe, and now Taunauk was paying the price.

"Do not despair, Helesys Byyra," Taunauk said in a voice not his own. She didn't recognize the young voice coming from him. "Taunauk is with us, but he is weary and resting."

"Does—Does it hurt him?" Helesys asked, surprising herself.

Taunauk's face was emotionless. "It strains him, but he will recover. The vessel of our people is resilient beyond compare."

Helesys nodded, trying not to look sullenly—knowing even then that she was failing in the task. She stared at her friend without knowing if he could see the distress on her face.

"Take care of him," she said. "He is nearly all I have." Helesys turned to Shawn—partly because she couldn't bear to look at Taunauk's blank face and because Shawn was also important to her.

The rogue smiled sheepishly. "I'm pretty fond of you guys, too."

Helesys and Shawn sat together on the ashen cliffs overlooking the scar. Though Taunauk sat beside them, he stared out over the landscape, feeling impossibly far away. Both the weaver and the rogue eyed Taunauk wearily.

"He'll be alright," Shawn said quietly. Then he sighed—long and wearily. "Back there... were you talking to that *thing?*"

Helesys recounted what the titan had said about itself, and about the queen. Shawn listened, eyes widening as the explanation went on.

"I had a feeling…" Shawn muttered. "But now I know. That thing was another Gatekeeper—another *dungeon*. An infant."

Helesys shook her head. "This doesn't make sense. It said the queen emerged from the crater, but we're inside the queen."

"She's both," Shawn said. "She *is* the dungeon, but she is also separate and controls it. I think once her kind eats enough, they gain mastery over their inner realms. Their, uh, trough, as that thing said. Here she is the canvas and the painter, the marble and the sculptor. …Or she was."

The Wolf King.

Helesys said, "I tried holding back the black dragon—if I had the spear, I might've succeeded for a time. I didn't dare try the spell on the titan back there… How in Movernus' name is the King controlling *Her?*"

Silence fell between them. Neither had an answer or could fathom a guess. Nor did they want to give breath to any possibility.

But even stronger than her disbelief was her revulsion. Finally, Helesys muttered, "She *ate* her kin."

"It's not that uncommon," Shawn replied. "There are creatures that eat their siblings in the womb. Don't ask me how I know that."

"That's… It's…"

"Evil?" Shawn asked. "Morality is a Terran construct. To animals, life is simple: There is eat or be eaten. To the old gods, well, it's about the same."

Helesys nodded. There was a part of her that knew Shawn was right. Even elves and humans could not agree on laws and society. But no thought could push aside the depravity of fratricide.

Helesys looked across the realm. "What about this place? Is this realm where the Queen was born? Is this her realm or her planet?"

Shawn contemplated this. "No… I think this is just the first realm she ate."

~

Helesys was so weary she would have slept, but none of them would risk so along the scar of the realm. There was no telling how long the infant titan would be kept at bay with the curse of cold fire.

Helesys turned her attention to the tiny jade lemur totem. Flying so quickly had drained about a third of its power, but if they could fly leisurely over the canyons, then its power would last longer.

She reached into the totem with her magical sight, hoping that she could restore some power to it. The lemur seemed opposite to her spear. The Gar of Shéslang did not hold power—it amplified power that flowed through it. The lemur absorbed power and distilled it. It did this mostly through ambient magic and with a long enough time. Helesys supposed she could feed power into the statue to accelerate the process, but she would need to do so delicately. Otherwise, she might damage it. Right now, she didn't have the time to experiment.

She narrated her dilemma to Shawn, to which he replied, "If you think it will get us across, I trust you."

Helesys called upon the jade lemur, and it sprouted from the stone. A moment later, the three climbed on its back and flew into the air.

The edges of the canyons faded from view, leaving only a pit of darkness beneath them. It felt as if the world had fallen away. There was no wind, no sound, not even cool breeze as they flew. Even the swirling purple sky was silent.

Dread filled her—not just from the darkness beneath or the otherworldly landscape. It felt as if they were teetering perilously on the edge of a cliff. Helesys chuckled at the dark humor. As pitiful as the analogy was, she had no other words for it.

Helesys called back to Shawn, "If this is the Queen's birthplace… then what lies beyond?"

Shawn chuckled from the back of the lemur. "I know a great many things, Helesys Byyra, but absurd questions don't have meaningful answers.

So, that's where they were going—into the absurd. To the heart of a god, to kill the king that had usurped her.

"Shawn…"

"Yes?"

"What if killing the Wolf King makes things worse?" she asked. "What if he's keeping the dungeon in check?"

Shawn was silent as they flew. "One problem at a time."

~

Helesys commanded the lemur to pace itself as they flew. She estimated its power would last through a normal day, but there was no way of gauging such time there. Instead, she kept her eyes on the canyon of darkness and tried not to think about the lemur's magic slowly dwindling.

She *felt* the center of the realm before she saw it. If the darkness beneath them was a wound in the realm, then it felt as if the inky black was flowing toward the center—being pulled toward it.

Like a hole in a leaking boat.

Even the still air above them seemed to flow toward it. Helesys thought it was her imagination until she saw the purple clouds swirling and coalescing in the distance.

Faster they flew—pulled along by forces beyond their control.

Then she saw it: A stain in the darkness. No; blacker than darkness. A hole in the world—in her vision.

It might've been a thousand feet across at most, yet it felt as if that hole could swallow all the realms she'd ever walked.

Helesys shuddered and wanted nothing more than to turn away. Deep-seated fear boiled within her—the kind she hadn't felt since she was a child. Like a rodent staring down a cat. She knew going in there meant that she would never escape. And deeper still, Helesys knew that even if they turned back now, they could not escape.

They were being pulled in. Eaten.

Stale air whooshed past them as they were pulled faster toward the hole. Even the made-thing lemur fought against the pull, straining to climb higher.

But it was no use. The three heroes screamed as the lemur plunged into the hole in the world.

Darkness surrounded them. The stained and jagged walls of shadow converged on a pinprick of nothingness. The wind died, and the world turned mute. Even the jade lemur's fur and beats of its wings felt distant—like Helesys might lose her grip. Even her own gasps for breath and beating heart were silent.

For a moment, Helesys dared look up—the opening receded from view, the swirling purple clouds shrinking. And in the tiny maelstrom, Helesys swore she could see eyes staring back.

Screams brought her back to the moment. A cacophony of shrieks rose from somewhere below. The darkness began to writhe.

Blots of nothing came for them—so dark against the absolute blackness that Helesys doubted her own sight. It was only out of the corners of her eyes that she could see them at all. Their bodies were small and winged like gargoyles brought to life. She thought back to the Cuckoo's illusions, but these were born of even fouler magic.

The jagged shadows reached at them, clawed at them, and the heroes met them in kind. Purple blasts, golden power, and silver contrails flashed in the darkness, each silent, yet each eliciting a shriek from the monsters. There were no sounds but otherworldly pain and rage.

The darkness grew oppressing, and the torrent of monsters threatened to swallow them. But in that desperate moment, Helesys felt her power growing—

Her own scream rising through the torrent.

The gargoyles that swarmed them were remnants—nothing more. They were pain and rage distilled from husks of things that used to be.

When Helesys had died on the Eternal Battlefield, she had been just like them. As the heroes plunged into incomprehensible horror, Helesys found comfort, for she had already been there. And she grew mighty.

She reached out to the gargoyles cloaked in crawling darkness and commanded them, *"DIE."*

And they did. So many gargoyles fell that it looked as if the walls themselves were crumbling.

The jade lemur tumbled over itself, the heroes clinging desperately to its back. The world spun. There was no up or down, there was only churning dark.

Helesys screamed, and hers was the only voice she heard.

~ ~ ~

NEXT TIME ON

*A BATTLEAXE AND
A METAL ARM*

Book 19:

Motes of Death

Available October 2022

Spoiler–Free excerpt from *BAMA 19*

By the time Helesys found the next door, the pair were soaked in blood. It was plain metal instead of stone, and unwarded. But when she pushed, it held firmly in place, metal groaning against her shoulder.

Behind her, Shawn's blades flashed against still more creatures and his cloak trailed with ghostly power.

Helesys bolstered her strength, then compounded it further with the Gar of Shéslang. Her breath swelled with strength and her bones grew heavy. Helesys leaned her shoulder into the door and *pushed*.

The lock snapped and the door swung open wide—slamming into the wall behind it. The hinges groaned and the door fell to the ground.

Helesys stepped through and the world grew hot. Steam filled the air and through it, Helesys saw bright molten slag. It fell in streams from the floors above and pooled in cauldrons and vats littering the floor. Along the ceiling high above, everlit candles loomed like stars. Clangs of smithing hammers and metal presses rang out like gongs.

This was no elven forge—it was a forge of men. The same one that Shawn had spent his mortal years in.

Helesys looked back, and found the metal door remade—closed and locked in place. There were no more horrid screams.

Beside her, Shawn looked over the room. "Guess we're in my memory now."

Shawn took a step, but Helesys grabbed his arm. "Shawn, what were those things back there? Where were we? Were those people?"

Shawn nodded. "They used to be."

To be continued October 2022

Thank you for Reading

I hope you enjoyed reading this story as much as I enjoyed writing it.

If you did, I would massively appreciate a short review on Amazon or your favorite book website. Reviews are crucial for any author, and a starred review or even just a line or two can make a huge difference.

It's especially true for the start of a series. Thanks and I hope you enjoy the next one!

Looking for more Engrossing Fantasy?

Check out more stories set in *Eluthiya*—the dark fantasy universe consisting of *A Battleaxe and a Metal Arm*, the ongoing short story collection *Tales from Another World*, and the monster hunter series *The Sword of the Gray Queen*.

What questions do you have about *A Battleaxe and a Metal Arm*?

If you've read this far, hopefully you'll read a bit further—both in this book and across the series. I'm not sure how most authors write serials and how much of it is flying by the seat of their pants, but that's not how I do things. For all the major questions that might come up in BAMA, I already have answers for 95% of them. Same goes for the major plot points, twists and climaxes. That might sound boring to some, especially some of you other authors who enjoy variations of writing into the dark, but I think having a solid blueprint is paramount to writing a long series.

So, what questions do you have about the story? Here are a few:

1) ~~What is the dungeon?~~ It's a soul trap of overwhelming size and power. But where did it come from? ~~Is it a force of nature or an ill-made weapon, or perhaps something else entirely?~~ The Dungeon is the Gatekeeper. She is both the marble and the sculptor. In the real world, it looks like a giant cloud with faces writhing just beneath the surface. Helesys speculates

that the reason no one remembers it is because it's so horrific their minds blot it out!

2) ~~Who was Helesys before she got trapped~~? We've learned that Helesys was both a soldier and was the oldest daughter of the elven Great House Byyra.

3) ~~Who was Taunauk before he got trapped~~? There was an omen of a blight in the Endroggen heaven, Accaelum. Taunauk is an Endroggen barbarian who was raised as a warrior and a vessel. His purpose was to one day free the trapped Endroggen souls from the Dungeon.

4) How well did they know each other beforehand?

5) ~~How did Helesys get her metal arm? Likely~~ through injury, amputation, and replacement. She was ~~likely~~ fighting in the Eternal War, the war of the Elves against the Shadowkind.

6) ~~Who is Shawn~~? He is a wisp from the plane of dreams. One who walks through the dreams of elves and humans, while being neither. He has lived as both a god and a mortal. His kind is on the run from the elder god, Nimicus.

7) Why does Shawn feel so familiar to Helesys and Taunauk? The group speculates that they were traveling together for unknown reasons. Shawn worries that they were tracking him. This could explain why Helesys and Taunauk are always reborn together, while Shawn was usually alone.

7) Who is the Wolf King and what sinister plans does he have for our heroes? How did he come to rule over the Dungeon? How does the Gatekeeper factor into all this?

8) Who is the mysterious voice encountered on the white sandy shores of Meridian? Why do they seek the death of the Wolf-King? ...And why did they choose the heroes? The Voice might be the Gatekeeper... but the truth is still unknown...

Did I miss any questions? Probably. Connect with me and other *BAMA* fans on social media and compare questions!

I've got plans. I've got answers. And I've got them on a drip-feed. Keep reading and expect to find out a little more to the mysteries with each installment. Hopefully, you're as excited about this series as I am.

Connect with the Author

If you want to stay up to date on the latest about Samuel's publishing news and blog, check out his website and consider signing up for his monthly newsletter.

www.SamuelFlemingBooks.com

Samuel can also be found on Reddit, Tiktok, and Facebook.

Samuel Fleming is a Science Fiction and Fantasy author.

He grew up in Maryland, spending most of his time swimming and writing. Swimming gave him a lot of time to daydream, so the two hobbies complemented each other well. Idle day dreams turned into stories, some of which stuck with him for years. These days he swims a little less and writes a lot more.

He loves a good story no matter the medium: Books, TV, video games, comics, tabletop RPG's, or podcasts–most of which he attempts to share with his wife and three kids, and occasionally on his blog.

www.ingramcontent.com/pod-product-compliance
Lightning Source LLC
Chambersburg PA
CBHW030650190726
48286CB00008B/2756